Breakfast

by Michèle Dufresne

PIONEER VALLEY EDUCATIONAL PRESS

Pickles is hungry.

Time for breakfast!
"Woof, woof," said Pickles.

"I am asleep," said Mom.

Time for breakfast!
"Woof, woof," said Pickles.

"I am asleep," said Dad.

Time for breakfast!
"Woof, woof," said Pickles.

"I am asleep," said Amy.

Time for breakfast!
"Woof, woof," said Pickles.

"I am asleep," said Danny.

"Woof, woof, **woof**! " said Pickles.

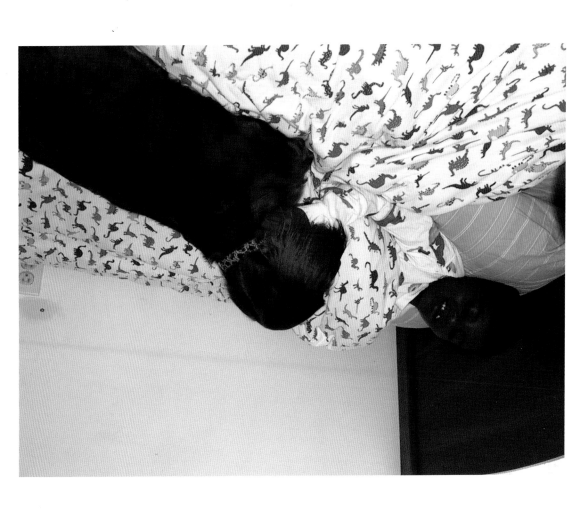

"OK," said Danny. "Time for breakfast!"